Snowy Bear

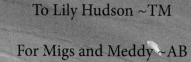

To Lily Hudson ~TM

For Migs and Meddy ~AB

Published as *Snow Bear* in Great Britain in October 2015 by Bloomsbury Publishing Plc

ISBN 978-1-338-15937-0

12 11 10 9 8 7 6 5 4 3 2 1   17 18 19 20 21 22

Printed in the U.S.A.   40

First Scholastic printing, January 2017

Art created with acrylic paint and colored pencil
Typeset in Lomba Book and Sketchley
Book design by Kristina Coates

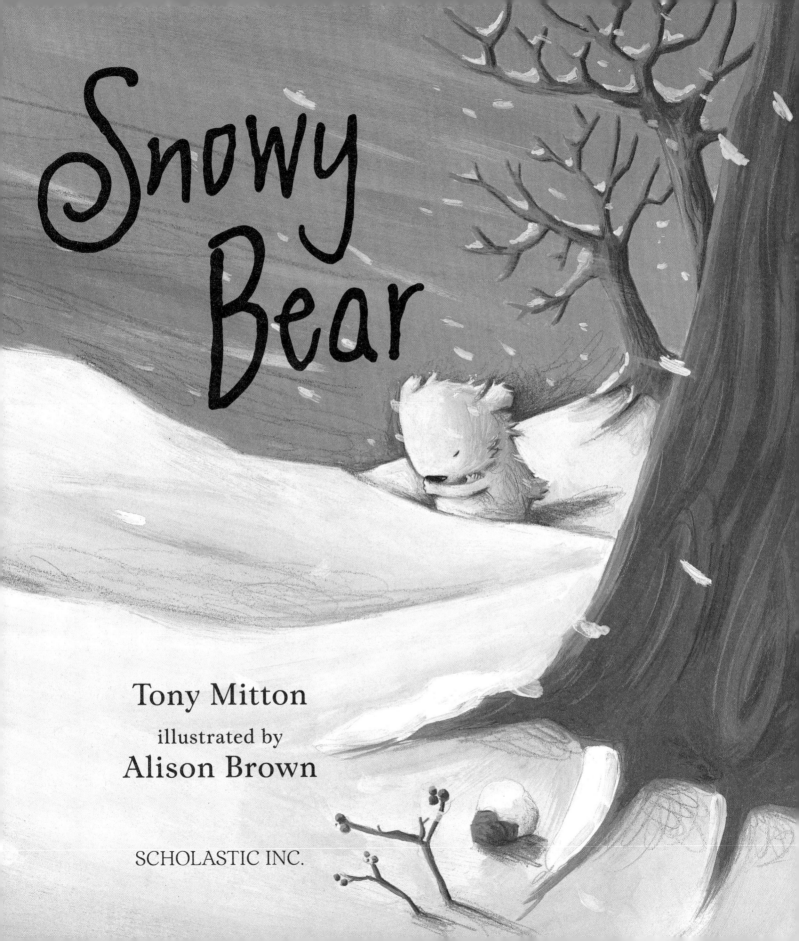

Snowy Bear

Tony Mitton

illustrated by
Alison Brown

SCHOLASTIC INC.

Here is a bear who has nowhere to go,
so he's plodding along through the cold winter snow.
Behind him his prints trace a long, weary line,
but ahead the snow's waiting, unbroken and fine.

If you were that poor little shivery bear,
you'd want to find comfort and warmth. Yes, but where?

He's spotted a hole, and it's dark, dry, and deep.
Perhaps it's a place where a cold bear could sleep?

"Oh, I'm sorry," growls Fox, "but there's no room to spare.
It's my den, and my litter of cubs is down there."

Snowy Bear climbs
up a crooked old tree.
There's a warm, cozy hole in it—
could it be free?

But tufty gruff Owl hoots,
"Tu-whit!" and "Tu-whoo!
My chicks are in there,
so there's no room for you."

Snowy Bear sighs. Then he trudges along.
"Oh, for a home!" is his sad little song.

But look! A small farmhouse
has come into sight,
a place that looks warm
in this cold world of white.

Perhaps there's a fire,
all glowing and gold,
to cheer a bear up
from the wintery cold.

A chilly breeze ruffles the fur on his cheek,
so Bear tiptoes in as the door gives a creak.

Inside it is warm, for the fire burns bright,
and Snowy Bear sees by its flickering light.

There by the window a child stands alone.
No one is with her. She's all on her own.
She looks through the window and out at the snow.
She's a little bit lonely, Bear seems to know.

She turns, for she senses him looking at her.
There Snowy Bear stands with his fluffy white fur.

She gathers him up, and she cuddles him tight.
And suddenly Snowy feels happy and right.

The little girl teaches him lots of new games.
Then they sit by the fire, gazing into the flames.
The girl gets a book, and she reads him a story,
till both of them start feeling sleepy and snorey.

The day's nearly over for girl and for Bear,
so they climb up the rickety, creaky old stair.

The girl takes the bear in her cuddly lap,
and they both snuggle down for a midwinter nap.

And that's where we'll leave them, both happily there—
a weary little girl and a tired Snowy Bear.
A cold winter day has now come to an end,
and a girl and a Snowy Bear both have a friend.